Anonymous

Picturesque Indianapolis

Anonymous

Picturesque Indianapolis

ISBN/EAN: 9783742825223

Manufactured in Europe, USA, Canada, Australia, Japa

Cover: Foto ©Andreas Hilbeck / pixelio.de

Manufactured and distributed by brebook publishing software (www.brebook.com)

Anonymous

Picturesque Indianapolis

PICTURESQUE INDIANAPOLIS.

---COMPLETE IN ONE NUMBER.---

J. R. Robinson, Publisher.  84 East Michigan Street,

INDIANAPOLIS, - INDIANA.

PREFACE

We present to the citizens of Indianapolis, and of the State of Indiana, PICTURESQUE INDIANAPOLIS, an elegantly illustrated historical souvenir of a great city. Sixty-nine years ago the Indian and buffalo roamed at will over the very ground where to-day stands the beautiful and prosperous Capital City of Indiana. The wonderful transformation in little more than half a century, all within the memory of many of our oldest citizens, of a dense, unbroken wilderness without a tree amiss, to the magnificent city of Indianapolis, with its 150,000 population, is living evidence of the energy and heroic endurance of the early pioneers of Indiana, their children and their children's children. The engraved pages of this work portray in their accuracy the grand march of American enterprise and civilization in the last half century.

In conclusion, we desire to state that in bringing PICTURESQUE INDIANAPOLIS to a finish, we are under great obligations for the encouragement and aid received from Mr. Frank Coffin, of the Indianapolis Cabinet Works; Mr. Albert Leiber, of the P. Leiber Brewing Company; Messrs. Kingan & Co., and Mr. John Faehr, Proprietor of the Spencer House, and we most earnestly hope that this work going out into the world may be the means of bringing to each and all of them a river of golden prosperity, that will flow on forever; and to every citizen of Indianapolis, and of the great State of Indiana, happiness and plenty.

THE PUBLISHER.

The City of Indianapolis.

THE old joke that made it one of the mysteries of nature, that "big rivers always ran beside big towns," is made a very positive fact in the close relation of large systems of transportation to large centers of industrial energy and development. Great railway centers are great manufacturing and commercial centers. Indianapolis is a notable illustration. She began a little scattered settlement of farmers, surrounded by swamps and permeated with chills and fever, on a river navigable only for canoes and pirogues, and no roads but bridle paths to the Ohio and White Water. She was ten years old before she had a thousand inhabitants, and for years afterward languished under the imputation of unhealthiness that repelled all but the most adventurous settlers. She passed her majority a country village still, with but one street and a lot of weedy lanes cork-screwed with cow-paths. A more unpromising condition never surrounded any town. It is not worth while to tell the steps and stages by which these crippling influences have been removed or modified. It will be sufficient to give the reader something like a correct idea of the condition the city has attained.

Indianapolis has now about 150,000 inhabitants and fifteen distinct lines of railway centering at her Union Depot. Several of these enter the city on lines common to two or more, and thus show less numerously than might be expected. The various lines collected here reach every county and county seat or important county town in the State. There is but one county of the ninety-two in Indiana that a resident may not leave in the morning, go to Indianapolis and transact ordinary business and return the same day. The average passenger business is from 10,000 to 13,000 arrivals and departures, a total annually of over 3,500,000.

The freight traffic may be conceived from the statement of the weekly movement of cars, loaded and empty. This runs from 18 000 to 23,000—sometimes more—an average of full 20,000, of which 15,000 are loaded and 5,000 empty. This is not the absolute average of the number shown by official statements to have been moved through or about the city on the Belt road and the connecting tracks, but it is a fair average of the weekly freight traffic, taking one week with another through the year. This average per week means over 2,000 cars a day, and over 1,000,000 cars a year, of which 750,000 are loaded and 250,000 empty. The loaded cars carry a freight of over 22,000,000 tons a year, and in a day of about 60,000. This is equal to the cargo of 60 ships of 1,000 tons each, and that is larger than the commerce of any city in the world except three or four of the largest. The Belt railway, circling the city, carries an average of 1,000 cars a day, or 30,000 tons, transferring them from one railway line or system to another. This exhibit of the railway or transportation facilities of Indianapolis, may be fairly balanced by a like exhibit of her industrial development. In 1880 the city had over 800 manufacturing establishments, great and small, employing over $10,000,000 capital, and over 10,000 hands, paying out $4,000,000 a year in wages, consuming $20,000,000 worth of material, and turning out $28,500,000 of merchantable products. In some lines of industry these amounts have since been doubled, with no change in natural conditions, and none of any kind that have not come about by an irresistible impulse of growth. A number of new ones have been added to these, a few old ones have declined and dropped out, and many old ones have been enlarged.

The astonishing discovery and utilization of natural gas for fuel and light has set Indianapolis far ahead of even the advantages she possessed before. Except Pittsburg, she is the largest city in the United States, or the world, that is or can be supplied with the best fuel ever known for the least price ever paid. Circling the whole northeastern territory adjacent to the city, at a distance and over a surface easily and cheaply traversed by piping, is the natural gas belt of Indiana; and into this four lines of pipe have already entered, and the city is already a great web of pipes reaching in every direction down streets and up alleys, filling a steam furnace on one block, a row of residences on another, and awaiting only on the movements of the workmen and the calls of residents, to provide every house with fuel at a fifth of the cost of coal. It may be easily conceived that such an addition to the city's attractions for judicious investments will draw a large share of attention her way.

In addition to these great and indestructible advantages, Indianapolis, in spite of her ill-repute for health in her earlier days, has now a hygienic record unsurpassed by any city of her size, or of any size, in this country or Europe. Her death rate is about 17 in 1,000. That is less than Philadelphia or Boston, or any other Atlantic city, or any lake city, can boast; and less than that of London, or Liverpool, or Paris, or Vienna, or Berlin, by far. A judicious sewerage system, extended gradually as opportunity offers, contributes largely to maintain these favorable hygienic conditions; a waterworks system aids all, and a health board looks closely after all transgressors of the regulations it has made. The city has also a system of free schools celebrated throughout the whole county for efficiency, with a fund sufficient to give a sound English education to every child in its limits. The high school holds a grade equal to that of many of the colleges of the West. Children of school age, 44,441.

The Indianapolis News.

As a product of journalism, THE INDIANAPOLIS NEWS is in many respects phenomenal, and in some it stands unique. Now in its twentieth year, it bears the distinction of being the eldest of all the afternoon two-cent newspapers in the West, taking Pittsburg for the dividing line between East and West. Four years after THE NEWS, came the "Detroit News." and after that, the evening papers of Chicago, Cleveland, Cincinnati, St. Louis and Louisville; all close students, and for the most part, slavish imitations of THE INDIANAPOLIS NEWS. The latter was not only a pioneer, blazing its own way upon original lines suited to its environment, but it has fairly kept the lead of all the afternoon papers, in respect to quantity and quality of matter furnished, joined to sustained ability of editorial comment; and, above all, in that lofty integrity in the pursuit of truth and sound policies—Municipal, State and National—which can not be turned aside by pecuniary consideration on one hand, or partisan motive on the other. The public recognition and patronage have been proportioned to the merit of the paper. While other afternoon papers, published in more populous centers have attained larger circulations, THE INDIANAPOLIS NEWS has recently attracted the attention of the whole country by successfully establishing its claim of larger circulation, proportioned to population, than any other American daily newspaper.

The Indianapolis Sentinel.

ESTABLISHED 1822.

JANUARY 28, 1822, Indianapolis people saw the first newspaper ever published in the city. The settlement was hardly two years old and the town had been laid out only about four months. There was no road to it—no way out of it, and no business in it. Everybody had been down with the chills the fall before. Starvation was held off by supplies brought on horseback from White Water or in canoes down or up White River. There was no mail and no post office. That first paper was the grand-father of the "The Sentinel," and was called "The Gazette." George Smith and Nathaniel Bolton, who had started the paper, sold it in 1830 to Alex. F. Morrison, who changed the name of it to "The Democrat." In 1841, the two Chapmans, George A. and Jacob Page Chapman, came from Terre Haute, purchased "The Democrat," and changed its name to the present one—"The Sentinel." The Chapmans changed the character of the paper a good deal, and made more of a newspaper out of it than it had ever been. In 1841, during the session of the Legislature, they made a daily edition of it, and kept it up until the close of the session of 1843-4, carrying a semi-weekly then, as had been done by their predecessors, until the permanent establishment of the daily—April 28, 1851.

In June, 1850, William J. Brown bought "The Sentinel," and the Chapmans retired from a position in which J. Page Chapman had achieved a national reputation. The campaign cry, "Crow, Chapman," was as frequent in Democratic meetings as any of the Whig cries of 1840 and 1844.

It originated in the imitation of rooster-crowing practiced by a prominent Democrat of Hancock County named Chapman, and had no reference to the editor of "The Sentinel," although it has always been supposed to have been originated by one of the Chapmans, who published "The Sentinel" at that period.

In August, 1852, Austin H. Brown published the paper, and his father was the leading editor. In 1855, Dr. John C. Walker and Charles W. Cottom bought out Mr. Brown, and later in the same year John S. Spann and John B. Norman bought the paper, the latter becoming editor. In 1856, Joseph J. Bingham, of Lafayette, purchased an interest, and the firm became Larrabee, Bingham & Co., until January, 1857, when John Doughty joined Bingham, and Larrabee retired. In 1861, Elder & Harkness bought the paper, and four years later Hall & Hutchinson succeeded to it, with the late Supreme judge, Samuel E. Perkins as chief editor. Richard J. Bright bought it in 1868, and Mr. Joseph Bingham again succeeded as the editor, a position which he had held with but little interruption since 1856, except during Judge Perkins' administration. He was longer the editor than any man who has ever held the position, except Mr. Bolton, and he did more than any one before him to give the paper the character of enterprise as a news collector and ability as a partisan champion, which it has since fully maintained.

In 1872 Mr. Bright sold to John Fishback and others, who formed the Sentinel Company, and this in 1878 was succeeded by Mr. John C. Shoemaker, who had finished his term of office as State Auditor. In his hands "The Sentinel" flourished as it had never done before. Col. Jacob B. Maynard was the editor. In July, 1886, Wm. J. Craig succeeded Mr. Shoemaker, who had, during his proprietorship, moved the paper into its present quarters near the State House, and equipped the office with a new press and entire outfit.

Mr. Craig, with "Gus" Matthews as editor, retained the paper until February, 1888, when it was purchased by the new Indianapolis Sentinel Company, which made great improvements in all the editions. They equipped the office with the latest improved machinery, reduced the price of the daily edition, and have built up the paper in circulation and influence until it has no superior in these respects in Indiana. It is enterprising and reliable as a newspaper, and fearless and able as a mouthpiece of Democratic opinion. "The Sentinel" is growing in popular favor every day.

THE LATE HON. THOMAS A. HENDRICKS.
Governor of Indiana. Senator and Vice-President of the United States.

The Indianapolis Journal.

ESTABLISHED 1823.

BOTH of the English morning daily papers of Indianapolis were founded in the first years of the city's history. The "Sentinel," on the 28th of January, 1822, about six months after Alexander Ralston had begun "laying out" the first plan of the place, and the "Journal," on the 7th of March, 1823, a little more than a year later than the other, but both before the removal of the State capital from Corydon to its present and permanent site. The first was originally called the "Indianapolis Gazette," but was consolidated in 1830 with the "Democrat," then recently started by the late Alexander F. Morrison, and called the "Democrat." It was purchased by the brothers Chapman in '41, and called the "Sentinel," remaining under that name till '65, when it was bought by Chas. W. Hall and called the "Herald," In '68 it was bought by Richard J. Bright and changed back to the "Sentinel," under which name it has remained ever since.

The "Journal," like its life-time associate, didn't start under the name it has so long been known by. It was called the "Western Censor and Emigrant's Guide" by Harvey Gregg and Douglass Maguire, who founded it. Like most papers of the frontier then and later, it was published as chance offered, between interruptions from impassable cow paths in the woods, high waters, failing mails and irregular supplies of paper. On the 29th of October, 1824, Mr. Gregg sold his interest to Mr. Maguire, and the latter, on November 16, sold it to John Douglass, State Printer, who had just come up from Corydon with Samuel Merrill, State Treasurer, and the State Archives, to inaugurate the capital in its new home. On the 11th of January, 1825, the name of the paper was changed to the "Indiana State Journal," which it still retains for the weekly edition, while the daily has taken the name of the "Indianapolis Daily Journal." No change has been made in the name of the weekly in more than sixty-four years, and none in that of the daily since it was established, nearly forty years.

Mr. Maguire remained as editor till 1826, and was succeeded by Samuel Merrill till '29. During this time General Thomas A. Morris, the real manager and victor of the campaign in West Virginia in the Civil War, served as an apprentice to the "art preservative" on the "Journal" before going to West Point. In '29 Mr. Maguire resumed the editorial direction of the paper and retained it till 1835, when he sold his interest to the late Samuel Vance B. Noel, who retained it till 1842, when he sold to Mr. Douglass, but in '43 bought out the whole establishment. Mr. Douglass retired from business permanently. During the absence of Mr. Vance, Mr. Douglass took Theodore J. Barnett as editor. He was a good speaker as well as a good writer, and so bitter in both characters as to provoke the equally prompt ascerbity of his Democratic rivals, the Chapmans of the "Sentinel," and for the first time the Indianapolis press was stained with the personalities and coarse language only too common in those days. Sometimes the rancor came near violent collisions, and once moved Mr. Barnett to draw a pistol on Page Chapman, father of the late General George H. Chapman. Mr. Kent succeeded Mr. Barnett as editor till March, '45, when John D. Defrees took the place, and the following year in February, '46, he bought out Mr. Noel, and retained both the proprietary and editorial control alone till the fall of 1854. He then sold to the first Journal Company, consisting of the late Ovid Butler, founder of the Butler University, James M. Mathes, Joseph M. Tilford and Rawson Vaile.

In the February of 1854, B. R. Sulgrove, who had been for some years a contributor to the paper, became associate editor, with all the editorial work to do, however. A daily edition of both "Journal" and "Sentinel" had been published during the Legislative sessions since 1842. In 1850 the official reports of the Constitutional Convention were published daily in the "Journal," and the daily edition has continued ever since. The "Sentinel" began a permanent daily in April, 1851. The first regular telegraphic dispatches were taken during the Crimean War in 1854, each office copying them from the reading of the telegraph operator. Mr. Sulgrove retained the editorial control till the summer of 1864, when he was succeeded by the late Judge H. C. Newcomb. The first reports of the proceedings of the night, which were published the next morning, were made by Mr. Sulgrove on the "Journal," and a little later by Austin H. Brown on the "Sentinel." The first verbatim reports of speeches, and editorials on the day's telegraphic news, were made in '54 by Mr. Sulgrove and Mr. Brown.

In the fall of 1864, the Journal Company sold to Mr. W. R. Holloway, Mr. Sulgrove having purchased a controlling interest in '58. In February, '65, the late James G. Douglass and A. H. Connor joined Mr. Holloway, who sold in 1870 to Wm. P. Fishback and L. W. Hasselman. Mr. Fishback sold to T. D. Fitch, and Mr. Hasselman's son, the present head of the job office, took an interest, and these held till '75, when Col. N. R. Ruckle obtained a controlling interest and failed in '76. Then Judge E. B. Martindale and W. R. Holloway bought the paper, Col. Ruckle retaining the job establishment, subsequently selling to Mr. Otto Hasselman, who still holds it. In 1880, John C. New & Son bought out Martindale and Holloway, and still retain the paper. Mr. Halford, the President's Private Secretary, was city editor for some years, later managing editor, and retained the latter position with marked success till he went to Washington with President Harrison. Charles M. Walker has been leading writer for a dozen years, contributing largely to the paper's reputation, as has Miss Anna Nicholas and Mr Wilkins, city writer, and Harry New, an excellent writer of humorous sketches and a very interesting correspondent. Thomas J. Steele is now managing editor, an old attache of the "Journal," and as reliable as men ever get to be George C. Hitt is business manager, but he is an admirable correspondent, too, and an effective editorial contributor. Col. New himself, when he cared to write, was an unusually vigorous and impressive addition to the editorial force.

The "Journal" was first published in an old frame building nearly opposite the site of the New York Store. In 1840, or thereabouts, it was taken by Mr. Noel to a frame building on the south side of Washington street, near the site of Albert Gall's carpet store. Some years later, about '46, it was removed to a three-story brick on the north side of Washington street, a little west of Meridian. Soon after this it was taken by Mr. Defrees to Pennsylvania street, in a three-story brick, since replaced by Fletcher and Sharpe's Block. Here it remained till 1860, when the Journal Company, which had bought the ground and built the house on the southeast corner of Circle and Meridian streets, put it there. In the winter of '67 it was removed to the Journal building on Market street and the first alley east of the Circle. It was then removed to the Martindale Block on Market street, opposite the postoffice, and then moved back to the Journal building in the northwest corner of Circle and Market streets. There it is now.

THE LATE HON. OLIVER P. MORTON,
The Great War Governor of Indiana.

INDIANAPOLIS—1820.
The Government Officers Preparing to Lay Out the Site of the City.
Engraved by the Boston Photogravure Co.,
From an Old Oil Painting in Possession of the City.

RESIDENCE OF THE LATE HON. JAMES BLAKE,
Corner of Tennessee and North Streets. Built in 1823—Still Standing.

*Engraved by the Bowen Photogravure Co.,
From a Drawing by Mary Y. Robinson.*

WASHINGTON STREET—1825.
View Looking West from Pennsylvania Street.

*Engraved by the Boston Photogravure Co.
From an Old Oil Painting.*

WASHINGTON STREET—1899.
View Looking East from Illinois Street.

OLD SEMINARY BOYS.

THE MARION COUNTY SEMINARY.
Erected 1832; Torn Down 1853.

Sketched from a Photograph by Mary T. Robinson.

———PRINCIPALS OF THE SEMINARY———

General Ebenezer Dumont.	1834.	Thomas D. Gregg.	1836.	Wm. A. Holliday.	1837–8.	James P. Safford.	1845-47.
Wm. J. Hill.	1835.	Wm. Sullivan.	1836-7.	James S. Kemper.	1838-45, still living.	Benj. L. Lang.	1847-53.

HENRY WARD BEECHER'S FIRST CHURCH IN INDIANA.
Cor. Market and Circle Sts., Indianapolis.

Engraved by the Boston Photogravure Co.,
From a Photograph by Rose.

RESIDENCE OF THE LATE HENRY WARD BEECHER—1845.
Built by His Own Hands. Still Standing on Ohio Street, Between Alabama and New Jersey Streets. Owned and Occupied by His Sister-in-law, Mrs. Katharine Bullard.

INDIANA'S NEW STATE HOUSE.
Cost $2,000,000. Occupies Two Full Blocks, Between Washington and Ohio, and Tennessee and Mississippi Streets. The Main Corridor, Running North and South in this Building, is 518 Feet in Length, and is the Longest Unobstructed Corridor Found in Any Building But One in the World.

MARION COUNTY COURT HOUSE,
Washington Street, Between Delaware and Alabama Streets. Cost $2,000,000, and is One of the Most Magnificent Public Buildings in the Country.

GENERAL BENJAMIN HARRISON, President of the United States.

GENERAL ALVIN P. HOVEY, Governor of Indiana.

HON. WILLIAM H. H. MILLER, United States Attorney General.

HON. JAMES N. HUSTON, United States Treasurer.

GRAND UNION STATION OF THE UNION RAILWAY COMPANY.
This Building Cost $1,800,000, and is Considered the Finest Structure of the Kind on the American Continent.

UNION RAILWAY STATION, INDIANAPOLIS, INDIANA.
Interior View of General Reception Room.

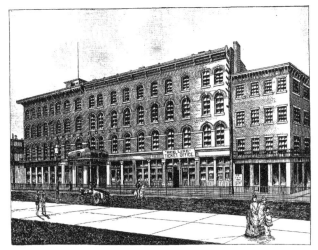

THE SPENCER HOUSE—JOHN FAEHR, PROPRIETOR.
Corner Illinois and Louisiana Streets, Opposite the Grand Union Railway Station, Indianapolis, Ind.

Engraved by the Boston Photogravure Co.
From a Photograph by Rose

Passengers on incoming trains can enter the Spencer House direct from the passenger sheds. The Spencer is one of most elegant and conveniently located hotels in the city. Street cars to all parts of the city pass the house every two minutes.

Regular Rates,	$2 00 Per Day.
Parlor Rooms,	2 50 Per Day.
Rooms with Bath,	3 00 Per Day.

The Spencer House is the only hotel in the city thoroughly equipped with fire escapes. The elevator runs day and night.

THE INDIANAPOLIS NEWS BUILDING.
Washington Street, Between Meridian and Illinois Streets.
Engraved by the Boston Photogravure Co.
From a Photograph by Rise.

ILLINOIS STREET—GRAND ENTRANCE TO SPENCER HOUSE.
Engraved From a Sketch by Harry C. Williams Holland.

VIEW ON PENNSYLVANIA STREET SUNDAY MORNING.
Looking North From Government Buildings.

Engraved by the Boston Photogravure Co.
From a Photograph by Rose.

Frank M. Talbott, Woodenware Store, Corner Pennsylvania and Market Street, Talbott Block.
White Sewing Machine Company, Exchange Block.
Henry Coe, Insurance, Second Floor, Corner Pennsylvania and Market Streets, Martindale Block.
Frank M. Hay, Real Estate and Loans, 59½, Room 18, Second Floor, Martindale Block.

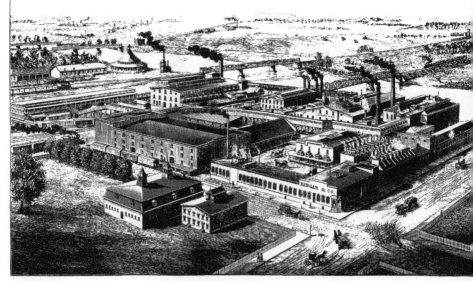

THE GREAT PACKING HOUSE OF KINGAN & CO., INDIANAPOLIS, IND., U. S. A.

P. LIEBER BREWING COMPANY, 504 to 520 Madison Avenue, Indianapolis, Ind., U. S. A.

*Engraved by the Bosse Photogravure Co.,
From a Drawing by Harry C. Williams Holland.*

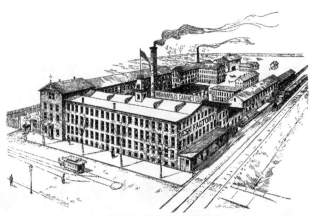

THE INDIANAPOLIS CAB'NET COMPANY'S WORKS.
The Largest Desk Manufactory in the World.

Stoughton J. Fletcher.   FLETCHER'S BANK, WASHINGTON STREET.   Francis M. Churchman.
Established 1839. A Half-Century of a Prosperous and Uninterrupted Business.

ed by the Boston Photogravure Co.,
From a Photograph by Bass

Fletcher's Bank Building is the Most Elegant and Complete Banking House in the United States.

THE WHOLESALE MILLINERY ESTABLISHMENT OF FAHNLEY & McCREA,
Nos. 140 and 142 South Meridian Street.

*Engraved by the Fenton Photogravure Co.,
From a Photograph by Rose.*

This great building also fronts on Louisiana Street, directly opposite the sheds of the Union Railway Station. The business was established in 1864, by Frederick Fahnley and Rollen McCrea. They employ forty clerks and salesmen and ten travelers.

RESIDENCE OF FREDERICK FAHNLEY, No. 200 North Meridian Street.
Engraved by the Boston Photogravure Co.
From a Photograph by Rose.

HON. ISAAC P. GRAY, Ex-Governor of Indiana.

RESIDENCE OF MR. W. J. RICHARDS, OF THE INDIANAPOLIS NEWS.
Corner of Pennsylvania and Seventh Streets.

RESIDENCE OF MR. JOHN C. SHAFFER, President Citizens' Street Railway Company,
No. 612 North Pennsylvania Street.

*Engraved by the Boston Photogravure Co.,
From a Photograph by Ruse.*

WATER GALLERY OF THE INDIANAPOLIS WATER COMPANY, Indiana Avenue.

*Engraved by the Boston Photogravure Co.,
From a Photograph by Ruse.*

THE NATION'S BABY—BABY McKEE.
President Harrison's Grandson.
*Engraved by the Boston Photogravure Co.,
From a Photograph by Potter.*

THE WHEN BUILDING AND INDIANAPOLIS BUSINESS UNIVERSITY.
*Engraved by the Boston Photogravure Co.,
From a Photograph by Ross.*

MASONIC TEMPLE,
Corner of Washington and Tennessee Streets.

Engraved by the Boston Photogravure Co.,
From a Photograph by Rose.

RESIDENCE OF MR. A. H. NORDYKE, 605 North Delaware Street.

MR. T. P. HAUGHEY'S COUNTRY RESIDENCE, "MAPLETON."

Engraved by the Boston Photogravure Co.,
From an Old Oil Painting by Cox.

VIEW IN WOODRUFF PLACE —Arthur B. Grover, Agent

WEDDELL HOUSE.
Illinois and Georgia Streets, Maj. A. W. Hanson, Proprietor.

FAIR BUILDING.
Illinois Street and Jackson Court.

Engraved by the Boston Photogravure Co.
From a Photograph by Rose.

W. C. Van Arsdel & Co., Wholesale and Retail Dealers in Dry Goods and Furnishing Goods, 109 and 111 South Illinois Street. Near Union Passenger Station.
L. Mayer, Clothing, Boots and Shoes, Gents Furnishings, Nos. 115 and 117 South Illinois Street. First Clothing House North of Union Station.
Second Story Fair Building, P. A. Sewald, Agent Mills & Gibb, New York City; Importers Dry Goods. No. 40 Jackson Place. Rooms 9 and 10, Indianapolis, Indiana. Opposite Union Depot.

LINCOLN PARK.
Bounded on the North by Seventeenth Street, on the East by Central Avenue, on the South by Fourteenth Street, and on the West by Meridian Street.

Engraved by the Boston Photogravure Co.,
From a Photograph by Rose.

MR. ROBERT MARTINDALE, Loans and Real Estate.
Agent Lincoln Park.

Engraved by the Boston Photogravure Co.,
From a Photograph by Rose.

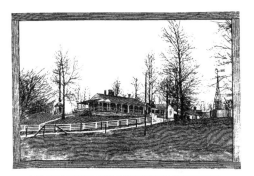

A CELEBRATED INDIANA STOCK FARM—TANGLEWOOD. Tanglewood House.

TANGLEWOOD TRACK AND STABLES, A. C. Remy, Proprietor, Indianapolis, Ind.

WESTERN HOMINY MILLS. Hall & Lilly, Proprietors.
Belt Railroad and Hadley Avenue, West Indianapolis.

Engraved by the Boston Photogravure Co.,
From a Photograph by Ross.

MILL MACHINERY MANUFACTORY.
Established 1851.

Complete large or small roller mills, with power included, furnished in one contract and price, using our automatic feeding roller mills and new style round reel flour dressers, and making a compact and easily set up outfit.

———WE ALSO MAKE A SPECIAL———
⋅❮FRONTIER ⁑ ROLLER ⁑ MILL❯⋅
———WARRANTED———

Costing in Running Order, Including Power and Building, Only $4,000.

All Machinery of the Highest Grade, and Our Prices Very Reasonable.

See our Rolls in the Washburn Palisade Mill, Minneapolis, Minn., American Mill Co.'s Mills, Nashville, Tenn., and Other Large Mills of the United States.

All are invited to state their wants and get our low proposals, either for new mills or to remodel buhr mills.   Send for new and interesting circulars.

———OUR ROLLS ARE LICENSED BY THE———

⟶Consolidated Roller Mill Company.⟵

NORDYKE & MARMON CO.,
Indianapolis.   ⚬   ⚬   ⚬   ⚬   ⚬   Indiana.

KINGAN & COMPANY,

PORK PACKERS

Indianapolis, * * * Indiana, U.S.A.

—CURERS OF THE—

"Reliable" Brand

—OF—

HAMS AND BACON.

Every Piece Guaranteed Perfect in Cure and of Uniform Quality.

—ALSO—

Pure Lard, Rendered in Kettles.

Hams and Bacon, Specially Adapted for the European Trade.

—ALSO—

PURE LARD.

National Accident Association

INDIANAPOLIS, IND.

Organized at Indianapolis 1887.

Accidents Will Happen in the Race For Life.

It Costs But Little to Insure Against the Loss.

Best Organization in the World.

DON'T FAIL TO PATRONIZE THE

A CRITICAL MOMENT

Reserve Fund,	$60,000.00
Assets,	$101,716.44

Benefits Paid for Accidental Injuries, $225,429.28
42 Claims for Accidental Deaths, 58,815.00
3,584 Claims for Weekly Benefits, 166,614.28

OFFICERS

M. HENNING,	President.
RALPH WORTHINGTON,	Vice-President.
JNO. A. WILKENS,	Secretary and Treasurer.
J. A. SUTCLIFFE,	Medical Director.
JOHN JORDAN,	Supervisor Industrial Department.

INDIANAPOLIS
MALLEABLE IRON COMPANY,
Indianapolis, Indiana.

MANUFACTURERS OF

Refined Air Furnace Malleable Iron Castings

Of Every Description, to Order.

QUALITY GUARANTEED

Agricultural Implement Work.

RAILROAD WORK

Makers of Castings for the Celebrated Ewart Detachable Link Belting.

CORRESPONDENCE SOLICITED

Van Camp Hardware and Iron Comp'y,

78, 80 and 82 South Illinois Street,

Indianapolis,   Indiana.

The Largest and Most Complete Stock in the West. In addition to our immense stock of SHELF HARDWARE, our TINNERS' STOCK Department, and CARRIAGE and Wagon Goods Stock, can not be surpassed.

—WE ARE—

HEADQUARTERS FOR Guns, Ammunition and Sportsmen's Supplies,

———IMPORTERS OF———

The Celebrated "RAOLA" Old-Style Roofing Tin.

The NICHOLS & SHEPARD COMPANY.
‹FACTORY AND HOME OFFICE›
Battle Creek, Michigan, U. S. A.

THE NEW VIBRATOR

NICHOLS & SHEPARD COMPANY.

W. S. McMILLEN,
Manager for INDIANA, KENTUCKY AND TENNESSEE.

Branch Office, 22 KENTUCKY AVENUE,
Indianapolis, - - **Indiana.**

⇒ SEND FOR ILLUSTRATED CATALOGUE ⇐

Coffin, Greenstreet & Fletcher,
PORK PACKERS,

Indianapolis. = = = = Indiana.

—CURERS OF THE CELEBRATED—

PRIMROSE
BRAND OF MEATS.

Primrose Sugar-Cured Hams,
    Primrose Sugar-Cured Shoulders,
        Primrose Sugar-Cured California Hams,
            Primrose Sugar-Cured Cottage Hams,
                Primrose English-Cured Breakfast Bacon,
                    Primrose Sugar-Cured Dried Beef.
Primrose Short Clear Sides, smoked or unsmoked,
    Primrose Short Clear Backs, smoked or unsmoked,
        Primrose Short Clear Bellies, smoked or unsmoked,
            Primrose Clear Pork,
                Primrose Bean Pork,
                    Primrose Rump Pork,
                      Primrose Pure Kettle-Rendered Leaf Lard, in Tierces, Buckets and Cans.

PORTABLE & STATIONARY Engines, Boilers, Etc.

Kept in Stock for Prompt Shipment — Engines Tested Under Full Load.

— MANUFACTURED BY —

Chandler & Taylor Company,

INDIANAPOLIS, **INDIANA, U. S. A.**

--- CIRCULAR SAW MILLS --- — OF — Best Design and Construction.

Side Cutting Mulay Saw Mills, — FOR — Large Timber and Light Power.

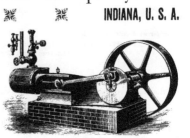

Haugh, Ketcham & Company,
IRON WORKS

Indianapolis. • • • Indiana, U. S. A.

Architectural Iron Work a Specialty.

Iron Fronts, Iron Roofs, Iron Stairs, Iron Furring and Lathing.

HAUGH, KETCHAM & CO. IRON WORKS
Erected the Iron Front for the Bates Block, Furnished the Iron Work for Marion County Court House, Indiana State House, and Similar Buildings, Public and Private, in all the

Large Cities of the United States.

CORRESPONDENCE SOLICITED

LAGER BEER BREWERY
Indianapolis, Indiana.

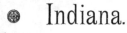

United States Internal Revenue
Deputy Collector's Office, 6th District, Indiana.
Indianapolis, Feb. 16, 1888.
I hereby certify that all of the monthly reports filed by **C. Maus** *in the office of the Collector of Internal Revenue since I have been in the office, show that* **Malt and Hops** *are the only ingredients used in the manufacture of Beer in his Brewery.*
James W. McGinnis,
Deputy Collector.

Bottled at the Brewery for Family Use

—ESTABLISHED IN 1864.—

Evans Linseed Oil Co.,

—Manufacturers of—

RAW AND BOILED LINSEED OIL

AND OIL CAKE MEAL.

—OFFICE—

Room 23, Vance Block,

Corner Virginia Avenue and Washington Street,

INDIANAPOLIS, - - - INDIANA.

WORKS, HAUGHVILLE.

J. A. HUNT, President.   J. H. SHIELDS.   W. H. SHIELDS, Secretary.

Hunt Soap and Chemical Company

MANUFACTURERS OF

SUPERIOR SOAPS

Best on Earth,

Great Anchor,

New Wrinkle,

Silver Star

Hunt's Borax Flake,
— OR —
Chip Soap.

Ferret Steam Boiler Scale Dissolver

701, 703 and 705 South West St.,

Indianapolis, - Indiana.

DATE	TO WHOM SOLD IN APRIL, 1889.	Chip Soap.	Ferret Steam Boiler Scale Dissolver.
		No. Lbs.	No. Lbs.
Apr. 1	E. S. Chatfield, Addison, N. Y.	100	
" 1	Union Fire Clay and Stone Co., New Lisbon, Ind.		25
" 1	S. C. Cougill, Summitville Ind.		25
" 3	Indiana Hospital for Insane, city	1722	
" 3	Central Chair Co., city		100
" 4	W. A. Johnson, Anderson, Ind	405	
" 4	Sinker-Davis Co., city	1479	
" 5	Famous Steam Laundry	600	
" 5	Indiana School for Feeble Minded Youth, R'hm'd.	443	
" 5	Hamilton County Infirmary, Carthage, O	486	
" 6	Bryce's Bakery, city		50
" 6	T. A. Conway, Carthage, O.		50
" 8	D. I. Wilson, Rushville, Ind	50	
" 9	Middletown Steam Laundry, Middletown, O	217	
" 9	Acme Steam Laundry, city	206	
" 11	Galt House, Louisville, Ky	2046	
" 11	Prospect Steam Laundry, Cleveland, O	668	
" 11	Sisters of St. Francis, Oldenburg, Ind	100	
" 12	Sinker-Davis Co., city		50
" 12	Star Steam Laundry, Louisville, Ky.	1082	
" 12	City Hospital, Louisville. Ky.	244	
" 12	Indiana Hospital for Insane, city	2582	
" 13	American Furniture Co., Batesville, Ind		100
" 13	Paul H. Krause, city	227	
" 15	New Denison Hotel, city	213	
" 15	Capitol Steam Laundry, Columbus, O	713	
" 15	N. C. Fink, Summitville, Ind		25
" 15	I. Stiulbaugh, Hamilton, O.		25
" 15	Efferson & Dodd, Ludoga, Ind	237	
" 15	Logansport Steam Laundry, Logansport, Ind	208	
" 16	Gem Steam Laundry, city		100
" 16	McKim & Cochran, Madison, Ind.	443	
" 16	Emerick, Paulini & Co., city	436	
" 17	P. S. Sorge & Co., Middletown, O	50	
" 17	J. J. Gutswiller, Cincinnati, O.		
" 18	National Home for Soldiers and Sailors	2408	
" 20	Sherman House, city		25
" 20	Deaf and Dumb Institute, city	931	
" 20	Middletown Paper Co., Middletown, O	524	
" 20	J. L. Walker, Steam Laundry, Kansas City	1118	
" 20	Conn Bros., Winchester, Ky.		25
" 20	Mess. Elcetlyt, Winchester, Ky.		100
" 20	S. P. Kerr, Winchester, Ky.		50
" 22	Sinker-Davis Co., city	929	
" 22	R. Johnson & Son, Madison, Ind		100
" 22	Troy Steam Laundry, Rectris, Neb.	216	
" 24	Dunlap & Coats, Columbus, Ind		50
" 24	Payne, Johnson & Co., Franklin. Ind		25
" 24	Greensburg Steam Laundry, Greeneburg, Ind.	50	
" 24	New Denison Hotel, city	203	
" 25	Hotel Ruffner, Charleston, W. Va	416	
" 25	Butler County Infirmary, Hamilton, O	650	
" 25	Acme Steam Laundry, city	218	
" 27	Blind Asylum, city	458	
" 27	Geo. Merritt & Co., city	31520	
" 27	Muncie Steam Laundry, Muncie, Ind	220	
" 27	W. F. Piel & Co, city	420	
" 27	American Steam Laundry, Cincinnati, O	1009	
" 27	G. G. White, Paris, Ky.		25
	Total No. pounds sold during month	49502	7720
	Total No. tons sold during month	24½⁰⁰⁄²⁰⁰⁰	3⁴⁴⁰⁄²⁰⁰⁰

THE NATIONAL SURGICAL INSTITUTE

Cor. Illinois and Georgia Streets,

Indianapolis. - - - - Indiana.

Founded by Dr. Allen in 1858. Incorporated by Drs. Allen, Johnson and Wilson, in 1869. For more than thirty years it has been rewarded by the most abundant success. The apparatus invented by Dr. Allen and used by this Institution have been copied and used in every civilized nation.

The Best Hotel Accommodations in Institute Building.

TWO years ago the management, realizing the necessity of increasing their facilities and improving their surroundings, entered upon a thorough renovation of the premises and the erection of an additional building. These improvements, now nearly complete, have been made with special reference to the work in hand. Four large buildings are now owned and occupied by the Institute, and its appointments are the most perfect of any similar institution in the United States.

The nursery for children under twelve years of age, presided over by trained nurses, has been entirely remodeled and supplied with new and suitable furniture, and a kindergarten (school) has been provided free for the children under treatment. A large and elegant treatment room, 45x80 feet, has taken the place of the old one, which had become inadequate. It contains $20,000 worth of new machines and apparatus, all of which were designed by Dr. Allen for the treatment of deformities, paralysis, etc. Connected with it is a thoroughly equipped gymnasium, with bowling alley, billiard table, swings, games, Indian clubs, dumb bells, etc., which are to be used by the patients in connection with their treatment. The hotel connected with the Institute has had its share of attention, having been repapered and painted throughout. The old system of heating has given place to steam, while natural gas is used for fuel. New and modern water closets have been put in, and the best of hotel accomodations can there be had under the same roof with the Institute proper.

More than 50,000 have obtained relief from its treatment.

Its patrons have come from every State in the Union, and from England, Scotland, Germany, Mexico and Australia.

More than 10,000 surgical operations have been performed at the Institute without a single death occurring from the operation, anesthesia or erysipelas.

Send three two-cent stamps for a book of 200 pages, which will be sent free, which gives a history of the work of the National Surgical Institute, with the names and addresses of hundreds who have been cured. This book puts the reader in the way of thoroughly investigating the merits of the Institute by placing in his hands the evidence of thousands who have been cured there.

It treats successfully every variety of deformity of the human body, such as Spinal Curvature, all manner of Deformed Feet and Hands, Crooked Knees, diseased and enlarged joints, White Swelling, hip joint Disease and deformities of the Face and Nose. A Special department for the treatment of Paralysis. Also, all Chronic Diseases.

Female Diseases Made a Specialty.

The National Surgical Institute is a permanent institution, with a capital of $500,000. The eminent success attained, the universal indorsement by all intelligent investigators, the thousands made happy by it, the magnanimous treatment of the poor, the moderate fees paid by the rich, and the frank and candid manner in which all are treated, have gained the UNIVERSAL CONFIDENCE and support of the people of the United States.

The Largest of the Kind in the World.

CPSIA information can be obtained
at www.ICGtesting.com
Printed in the USA
LVHW090916250420
654406LV00002B/637